THE BULLY BROTHERS AT THE BEACH

by Mike Thaler • Illustrated by Jared Lee

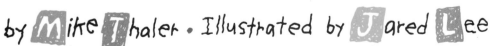

SCHOLASTIC INC.
New York Toronto London Auckland Sydney

For Juwanda Ford,
in thanks and appreciation
—M.T.

To my little nieces,
Stephanie and Cassy
—J.L.

ISBN 0-590-47802-8

12 11 10 9 8 7 6 5 4 3 2 1   6 7 8 9/9 0 1/0

Printed in the U.S.A.   23

First Scholastic printing, April 1996

Bubba and Bumpo loved the beach.
So when Miss Winky, their teacher, announced
a field trip to the seaside, they were thrilled.

On the day of the trip, everyone brought a beach bag.
Freezer had twenty peanut butter sandwiches in his.
Stats had baseball cards.
Cynthia Melnick had three encyclopedias.
Rodney Fish had eight tubes of sunscreen.

And Goody had a pink shovel and matching pail.
Bubba and Bumpo wouldn't show anyone
what was in *their* beach bags.
"You'll find out," said Bumpo.
"You sure will," smiled Bubba.

When they arrived at the beach,
everyone changed into their bathing suits,
and ran down to the water.

Freezer ran right in with a big splash.
Stats, Cynthia, and Goody cautiously followed.

Rodney stood at the edge, dipping his toe.
"Are you going in?" said Bumpo.
"Eventually," said Rodney, putting on more sunscreen.
"We'll help you," Bubba and Bumbo smiled.
Bubba took one arm.
Bumpo took the other.
And they carried Rodney into a big wave.

"You're such bullies," said Cynthia, treading water.
Bubba and Bumpo splashed her.
"Look out for waves," they said.
Just then Freezer floated by on his back.
"Ship ahoy," yelled Bubba,
doing his Long John Silver imitation.
"Why don't you grow up," shouted Cynthia.
They splashed her again.

Miss Winky blew her whistle.
"You boys come out of the water immediately!"
She took hold of Bubba's ear.
She took hold of Bumpo's ear.
And led them back to the beach.
"Now you boys stay here,
until you can behave yourselves."
Then Miss Winky went into the water.

"What a drag," said Bumpo.
"What a drag," said Bubba, picking up Goody's shovel. "Let's bury some treasure."
They dug a big hole and buried everyone's bags in the sand.

"*Now* let's play Jaws," said Bubba, reaching into his bag.
"De dum . . . de dum," hummed Bumpo,
reaching into his.
Hiding something gray behind their backs,
they snuck back into the water.

"Goodness gracious!" cried Miss Winky.
"Sharks!" yelled Rodney.
Everybody headed for the shore.

The two sharks followed behind them.
Everyone ran out of the water screaming!

The two sharks bobbed up and down.
"I never saw Freezer move so fast,"
laughed one of the sharks.
"And Rodney turned whiter than usual,"
giggled the other.

Suddenly a big net fell over the sharks,
and they were lifted out of the water.
The lifeguard had radioed a coast guard boat
at the first sighting of sharks, and Bubba and
Bumpo now hung in their net.

"What kind of sharks are those?" asked the captain.
"They look like man-eaters," said the first mate.
"No, we're not," cried Bubba.
"We're vegetarians," shouted Bumpo.

"What should we do with them?" asked the captain.
"We better harpoon 'em," said the first mate.
"We're not sharks," cried Bubba, tears streaming
down his cheeks.
"We're boys with cardboard fins," bawled Bumpo.
"Well," said the captain, lifting the net over the
beach and dumping the boys out.
"So you are."

Miss Winky bravely walked forward, and took each shark by the ear.
The captain waved good-bye as the boat moved out to sea.
"You boys come with me," said Miss Winky, taking Bubba and Bumpo back to the others.

Together, all the kids dug a big hole in the sand, and buried Bubba and Bumpo up to their chins. "Now," said Miss Winky, "stay put."

"Where's my bag?" said Freezer.
"And ours," said all the other kids.
"We'll never tell," said the heads sticking out
of the sand.
"There's an ancient torture," said Rodney,
"where you bury people up to their chins in sand,
and pour honey over them."

"We could use ice cream," said Cynthia.
"And then the ants come and eat their brains,"
smiled Stats.
"It wouldn't be much of a meal," said Cynthia.

"Okay, okay," said the heads, "we buried your bags right behind you."

Everyone dug up their bags.

"My sandwiches are full of sand," said Freezer.
"That's why they're called SAND-wiches,"
said Bubba's head.
Bumpo's head laughed.

"Well," said Miss Winky, "you two can eat Freezer's SAND-wiches, while the rest of us go up to the snack bar and get hot dogs, hamburgers, and lemonade."

"That's not fair," said Bumpo, his nose resting on a peanut butter sandwich.
"And besides," said Cynthia, "they don't allow SHARKS at the food stand."

And off went the class, waving good-bye.

"Some people just don't appreciate a little kidding around," said Bumpo. "No," said Bubba, blowing his nose on Bumpo's sandwich.

Bubba looked at Bumpo.
Bumpo looked at Bubba.
They both looked at the peanut butter sandwiches.